The Dead Sea Squirrels Series

Squirreled Away

Boy Meets Squirrels

Nutty Study Buddies

Squirrelnapped!

Tree-mendous Trouble

Whirly Squirrelies

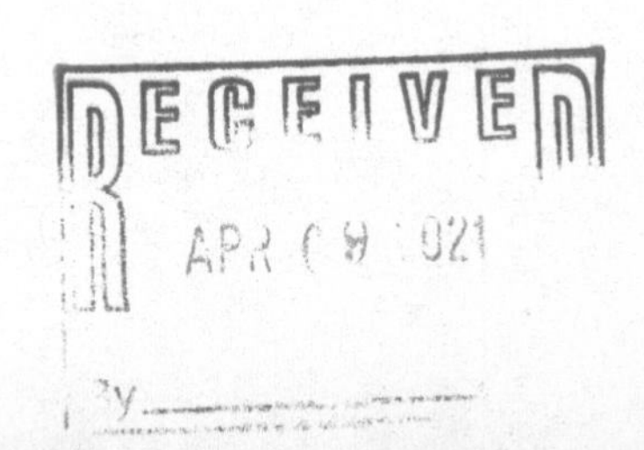

Whirly Squirrelies

Mike Nawrocki

Illustrated by Luke Séguin-Magee

Tyndale House Publishers
Carol Stream, Illinois

Visit Tyndale's website for kids at tyndale.com/kids.

TYNDALE is a registered trademark of Tyndale House Publishers. The Tyndale Kids logo is a trademark of Tyndale House Publishers.

The Dead Sea Squirrels is a registered trademark of Michael L. Nawrocki.

Whirly Squirrelies

Designed by Libby Dykstra

Edited by Sarah Rubio

Published in association with the literary agency of Brentwood Studios, 1550 McEwen, Suite 300 PNB 17, Franklin, TN 37067.

For manufacturing information regarding this product, please call 1-800-323-9400.

For information about special discounts for bulk purchases, please contact Tyndale House Publishers at csresponse@tyndale.com, or call 1-800-323-9400.

Library of Congress Cataloging-in-Publication Data

Names: Nawrocki, Michael, author. | Séguin Magee, Luke, illustrator.
Title: Whirly squirrelies / Mike Nawrocki ; illustrations by Luke Séguin-Magee.
Description: Carol Stream : Tyndale House Publishers, Inc., 2020. | Series: The Dead Sea squirrels | Summary: When it comes to drones and video games, fifth-grader Michael and Merle, a 2000-year-old talking squirrel, have very little self-control.
Identifiers: LCCN 2019024361 (print) | LCCN 2019024362 (ebook) | ISBN 9781496435187 (trade paperback) | ISBN 9781496435194 (kindle edition) | ISBN 9781496435200 (epub) | ISBN 9781496435217 (epub)
Subjects: CYAC: Squirrels—Fiction. | Drone aircraft—Fiction. | Video games—Fiction. | Self-control—Fiction. | Christian life—Fiction.
Classification: LCC PZ7.N185 Wh 2020 (print) | LCC PZ7.N185 (ebook) | DDC [Fic]—dc23
LC record available at https://lccn.loc.gov/2019024361
LC ebook record available at https://lccn.loc.gov/2019024362

Printed in the United States of America

26 25 24 23 22 21 20
7 6 5 4 3 2 1

To the wonderful team at Tyndale who helped bring the squirrels to life—most especially to my editor, Sarah, who helped this first-time author look like he knew what he was doing.

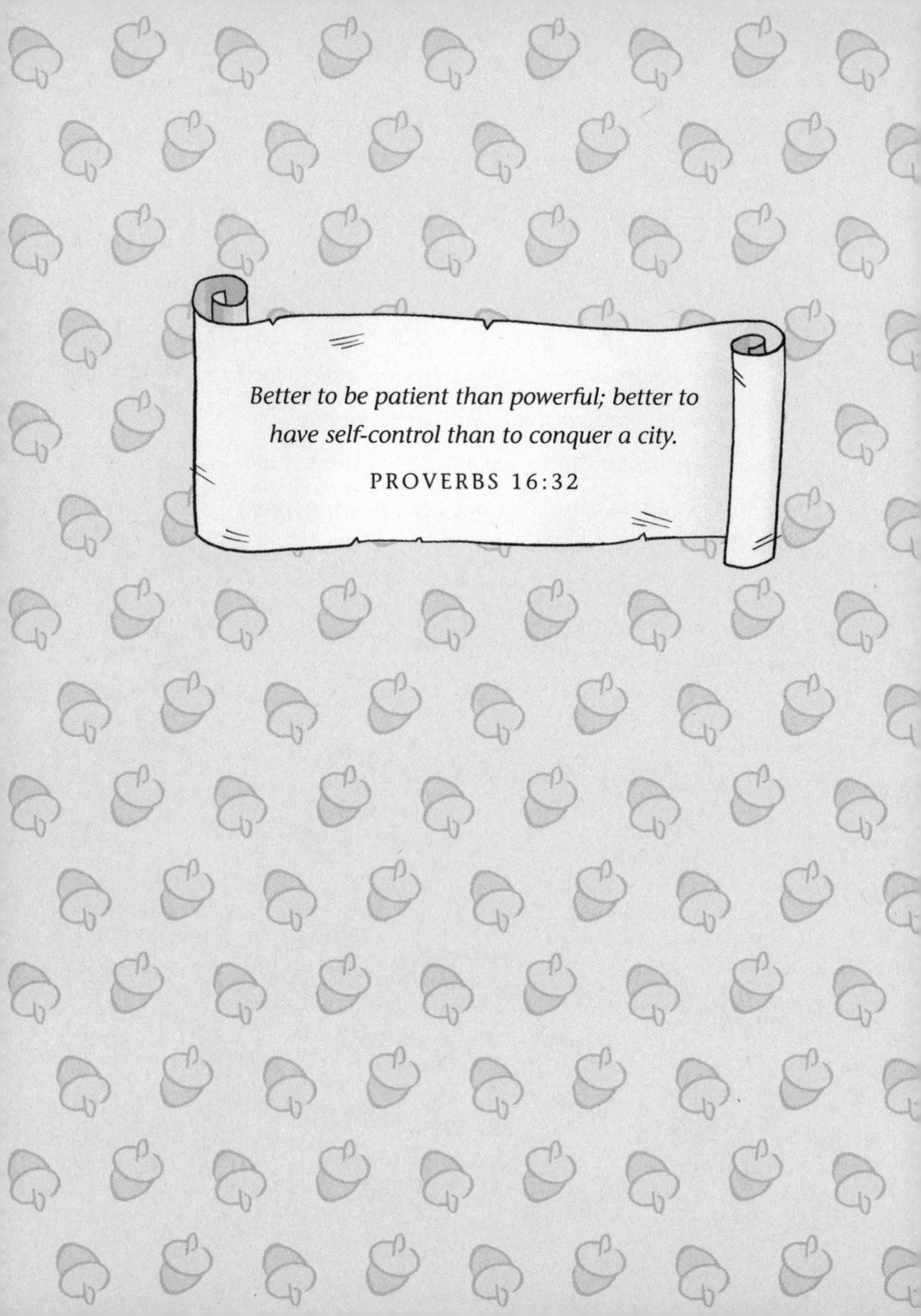
Better to be patient than powerful; better to have self-control than to conquer a city.
PROVERBS 16:32

BEFORE WE START...

Who are the Dead Sea Squirrels?

Soon the two salty squirrels are hot, thirsty, and desperate for shade. Then they spot a cave.

Merle's sense of adventure lures him into the cave, despite Pearl's protests.

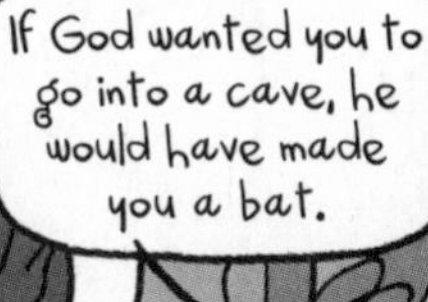

1,950 YEARS LATER
Ten-year-old Michael Gomez is spending the summer at the Dead Sea with his professor dad and his best friend, Justin.

While exploring a cave (without his dad's permission), Michael discovers two dried-out, salt-covered critters and stashes them in his backpack.

Michael sneaks the squirrels back home with him to Tennessee.

Up and kicking again after almost 2,000 years, Merle and Pearl Squirrel have great stories and advice to share with the modern world.

They are the Dead Sea Squirrels!

WOOO WOOO
WOOO!

CHAPTER 1

WALNUT CREEK, TENNESSEE
PRESENT DAY (MONDAY)
11:32 P.M.

A loud thump on Michael Gomez's bedroom window was followed immediately by the shriek of the burglar alarm Michael's dad had installed to help protect Merle and Pearl Squirrel from the man in the suit and sunglasses, a mysterious agent working for a collector of ancient artifacts. He wanted to bring Merle and Pearl back to the Dead Sea, which was the last place on earth they wanted to be. The ancient squirrels preferred modern-day

Tennessee with its abundance of nuts and HVAC (Heating, Ventilation, and Air-Conditioning). After having spent nearly 2,000 years preserved in salt in a dusty desert cave, who could blame them?

Michael sat straight up in bed and looked over at Merle and Pearl, nestled comfortably in their sawdust in the enormous converted hamster cage Mrs. Gomez had constructed for the squirrels as a permanent home in Michael's room, complete with running water and shiplap.

"Shhh . . . ," Merle shushed, still half asleep, waving his paw in the air in a poor attempt to shoo away the annoying alarm sound.

Dr. Gomez popped his head into the room, dressed in pajamas and slippers and looking like he'd also been asleep. "Everyone okay?!" he asked urgently.

"Yeah, we're fine," Michael responded.

"Shhh . . . ," Merle repeated as the alarm continued to sound.

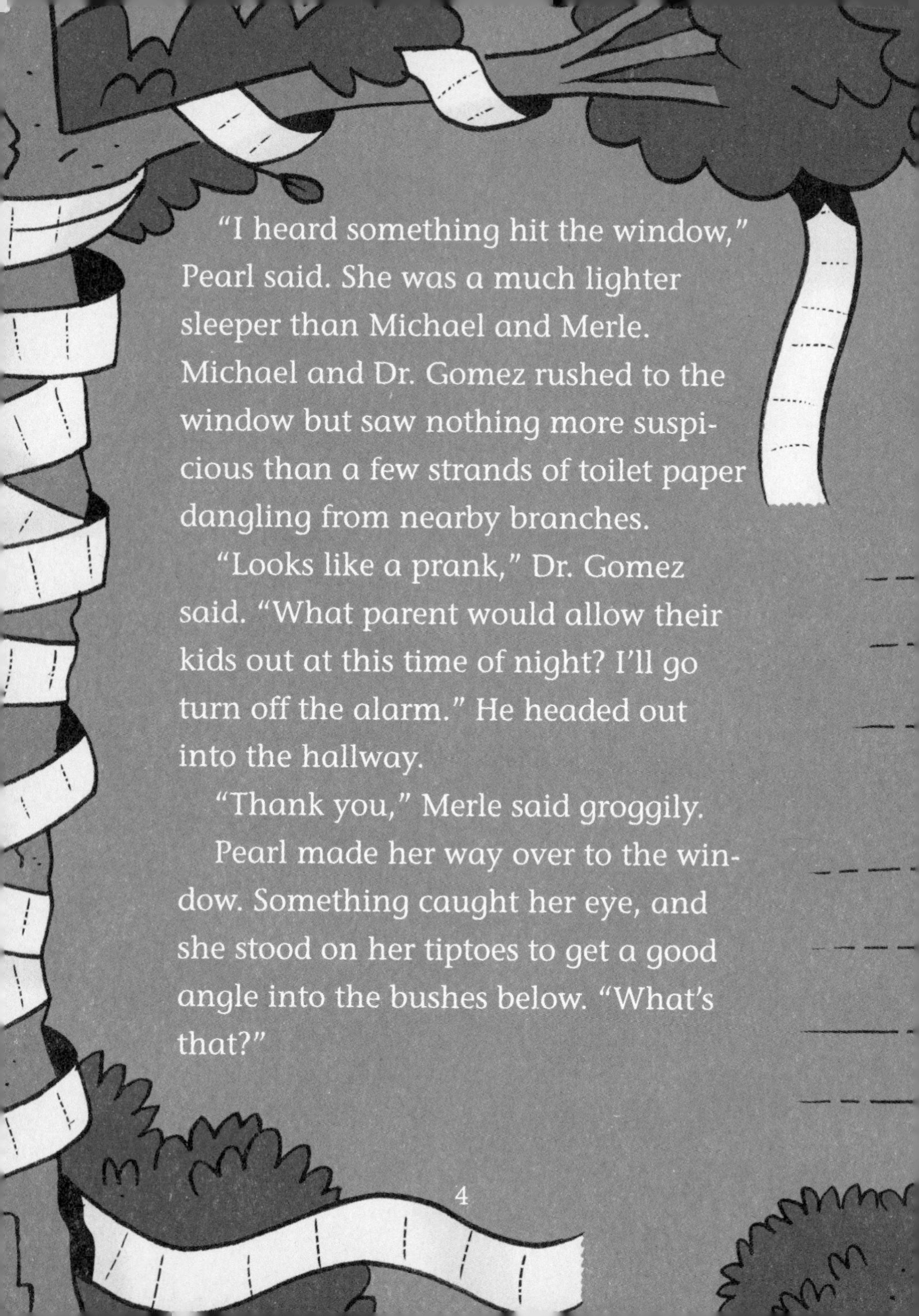

"I heard something hit the window," Pearl said. She was a much lighter sleeper than Michael and Merle. Michael and Dr. Gomez rushed to the window but saw nothing more suspicious than a few strands of toilet paper dangling from nearby branches.

"Looks like a prank," Dr. Gomez said. "What parent would allow their kids out at this time of night? I'll go turn off the alarm." He headed out into the hallway.

"Thank you," Merle said groggily.

Pearl made her way over to the window. Something caught her eye, and she stood on her tiptoes to get a good angle into the bushes below. "What's that?"

Michael slid the window open as the sound of the alarm cut out. "It looks like a . . . drone?" Sure enough, a drone lay sideways in the bushes, buzzing limply like an injured bee, its propellers tangled in toilet paper. He reached down and picked it up.

"Is everyone okay down there?" Bob the squirrel called (in squirrel) from the large walnut tree just outside Michael's window. Bob, along with his wife, Mary, and their friend Larry, had just met Merle and Pearl earlier that day.

"We're fine, Bob, thank you!" Pearl chirped in squirrel. "Just trying to figure out what it was that ran into our window."

"I think it might belong to those guys." Bob pointed from his perch on high. Some distance off stood Walnut Creek Elementary's resident bully, fourth-grader Edgar, along with his two minions, Pete and Bruce.

"They've been decorating your home," Mary added, popping out from a knothole in the tree. "It's lovely the way the paper blows in the wind."

Edgar realized he'd been spotted. "Give me back my drone, Gomez!" he hollered.

"Not when you're using it to TP my house!" Michael shouted back.

The porch lights clicked on, and the voice of Dr. Gomez rang out. "You! Boys! What are you doing?" This sent the three delinquents scrambling. In his panic, Edgar dropped the drone's remote control on the lawn.

"That's right! Run away!" Michael called out. "And don't come back!"

"Michael." His dad's voice came from the porch. "Please clean this mess up after school tomorrow."

"Aw, man!" Michael responded.

"Shhh . . . ," Merle, still half asleep, said again from his bed.

CHAPTER 2

"This is amazing!" a well-rested Merle exclaimed the next morning, inspecting the sleek drone resting on the wooden floor of Michael's bedroom.

"You didn't seem to care at all about it last night," Pearl said from her tiny dressing room in their squirrel mansion.

"I was trying to sleep while you two were droning on about 'drone this and drone that,'" Merle replied, proudly smiling at his pun. "I never imagined it would be so spectacular! What does it do?"

"It flies." Michael pointed to the four blades atop the drone. "These propellers spin around really fast, and it lifts off the ground. You control it with this remote." Michael showed Merle the drone remote control that Larry the squirrel had retrieved from the yard.

"Like a bird?" Merle asked in wonder.

"Yup. Just like a bird." Michael clicked on the remote, and the propellers started up. Merle jumped back in surprise as the drone rose off the ground. With two swipes of the joystick, the drone lurched forward, stopped short of hitting the wall, then zipped back in the opposite direction toward the door.

Merle laughed like a four-year-old opening a gift on Christmas. "Can I try?"

"Sure. But try not to run into anything," Michael said as the door opened and Justin walked in, the drone hovering near his face.

"Cool drone," Justin commented. "Where'd you get it?"

"Captured it from Edgar last night," Michael said. "He was using it to TP our house."

"That was going to be my next question," Justin said. "Your house looks so flow-y."

Pearl gazed out the window at the billowing strands of white. "I think it's pretty."

"I think cleaning it up is gonna stink," Michael replied. "Come on, Justin." He and Justin headed off to school, waving goodbye to Merle and Pearl.

With the family cat, Mr. Nemesis, safely locked in Michael's sister, Jane's, room, Merle spent most of the morning flying the drone around the house. He managed not to break anything as he was getting the hang of the remote, but he did bump into a few things, including the on button of the television.

"*Glaucomys volans,* or the Southern flying squirrel, can jump from tree tops and glide like a bird on the wind," the nature documentary announcer said in his buttery English accent, as a flying squirrel leaped off a branch and sailed through the treetops. Merle couldn't believe his eyes.

"Pearl! Look at this!" Merle yelled, the drone

hovering above his head. "I had no idea we had flying cousins!" As it turns out, flying squirrels can be found in many different parts of the world, just not the part Merle and Pearl were from.

"Would you look at that . . . ," Pearl marveled. "It's more of a glide than a fly, though."

"It's still amazing! I wonder if I've got any flying squirrel blood in me?" Merle wondered, eyeing the drone.

"Don't get any silly ideas," Pearl warned.

"Too late," Merle said.

CHAPTER 3

Michael and Justin successfully avoided Edgar upon their arrival at Walnut Creek Elementary School. In their opinion, confronting Edgar was something to be avoided at all costs. That's the main reason they walked to school. Riding the bus would be much easier and much faster, but their bus was also Edgar's bus.

"You know he's going to want his drone back, even if he has to pound it out of you," Justin warned as the two friends crouched behind the bushes at the entrance to the school.

"Not until he apologizes for TP-ing

my house," Michael whispered defiantly.

"Are you nuts?" Justin asked. "He's not going to apologize! He's too big to apologize."

Just then Michael and Justin's other best friend, Sadie, passed by with her friend Maddie.

"Did you hear?" Sadie was saying excitedly. "*Super Squish Squids 3* releases tonight!"

Michael's fear of Edgar was immediately replaced by elation. "TONIGHT?!!!" he shouted, popping out of the bushes and scaring the girls half to death. They screamed in unison. Sadie whipped off her back-pack and whacked Michael over the head with it in one swift ninja move.

Michael protested.

"Don't scare us like that!" Sadie answered.

"Sorry, I didn't mean to."

"We were hiding from Edgar," Justin explained.

"When did you hear about *Super Squish Squids 3*?!" Michael asked. It was his favorite video game of all time.

"This morning," Sadie answered proudly. *Super Squish Squids* was also her all-time favorite game. Being the first kid at school with this news gave Sadie the upper hand in her *Super Squish Squids* rivalry with Michael.

"Aw, man. I can't wait to get home!" Michael said.

"Same here," Sadie declared.

The friends made their way to class, putting off the inevitable showdown with Edgar until lunchtime.

"Where's my drone, Gomez?!" Edgar demanded, approaching the fifth-grade lunch tables with his two minions. Michael had been counting on his classmates for protection, and they did not disappoint. At least ten kids slid their chairs back and stood up.

"The one you used to TP my house?" Michael asked boldly.

"Um . . ." Edgar stuttered. "Yeah?"

"You can have it back if you apologize," Michael insisted.

Edgar sneered. "I'm too big to apologize."

"I told you," Justin whispered.

Michael stared Edgar down. "No apology, no drone."

As Edgar looked around at Michael's backup posse, he knew he'd been beat. "All right. Sorry. Gimme back my drone."

It wasn't much of an apology, but Michael was surprised to hear it none-theless. "Also," he added nervously, "no beating me up once I hand it over."

"Grrrr . . . ," Edgar conceded as he retreated to the fourth-grade tables.

"Cool. I'll bring it to school tomor-row," Michael called out.

CHAPTER 4

Merle stood over the drone, which rested, lifeless, on Michael's bed. "I think I broke it."

"You ran it into too many things," Pearl sighed.

"Just four!" Merle fretted.

"Michael told you not to run it into *anything*."

"He told me to *try* not to run it into anything, which is exactly what I did."

Just then, the door opened. Merle turned, looking nervous and guilty, like a dog who had gotten into the garbage while his owner was out.

"Hey, guys! What's up?" Michael asked.

"Not the drone," Pearl said.

Merle jabbed her in the side with his elbow.

Michael inspected the drone and fiddled with the remote. "Hmm," he said. "Must be out of battery."

Michael spent the next ten minutes explaining to the squirrels what electricity is and how batteries store a charge until it is all used up. "I'm sure Edgar has the charger. He'll recharge the drone when I give it back."

Merle wasn't sure he totally understood the explanation but was relieved that he hadn't broken the drone. "Well, it was fun while it lasted," he sighed.

"It's for the best, dear," Pearl consoled him. "There's no telling what kind of trouble you could have gotten into."

SCIENCE
SCIENCE

CHAPTER 5

Michael bolted to the door to greet his mom when she arrived home from a day at the science museum with Jane. "Mom! So great to see you! Did you have a good day? Can I help you carry anything from the car? Jane, you look nice today," he babbled.

Mrs. Gomez glanced suspiciously at her son. She knew Michael well enough to know that this kind of nice usually meant he wanted something.

"What do you want?" Jane asked, beating her mom to the punch.

"Nothing," Michael replied sharply. An awkward silence followed as Mrs. Gomez continued to look sideways at

Michael. Finally, he confessed, “Okay. Maybe I do want a little something. *Super Squish Squids 3* came out today, and I really, really, *really* want it. It’s the best game ever. I’m amazing at *Super Squish Squids 1* and *2*, and *3* has like 20 more caves and a giant unsquishable squid and an evil octo-pus. Sadie’s getting it tonight, and if I don’t get it too, she’ll get way ahead of me, and I will totally freak out!” In Michael’s mind, this was an airtight argument. However, Mrs. Gomez was not convinced.

“How much does it cost?” she asked.

“It’s only $40!” Michael gushed.

“*Only* $40? Since when do *only* and *$40* appear in the same sentence of a ten-year-old?” Mrs. Gomez inquired.

“I have $15, and you can make it an

early birthday *and* Christmas present," Michael pleaded.

Under the word *persistence* in some dictionaries, you will find the picture of a ten-year-old who wants a video game. The same picture can also be located under the words *badger, irritate, annoy,* and *discommode*. After a number of failed refusal attempts, Mrs. Gomez finally gave in.

"All right," she conceded. "*After* you do your homework and *after* you clean up the toilet paper and *after* you eat your dinner, we can download *Squishy* . . . what?"

"*Super Squish Squids 3*." Michael smiled as he gave his mom a super hug.

CHAPTER 6

Shortly after Michael and the squirrels finished un-TP-ing the house, as the sun was setting, a white sedan pulled silently up to the Gomezes'. A shadowy figure exited the car and placed a mysterious package on the porch.

If you've ever waited for a package to arrive, you know that they are almost always delivered during the day, so if this delivery strikes you as fishy, you're probably right.

"Hey, buddy, it's time for bed," Dr. Gomez announced at 8:30 as Michael squished squids in the living room.

“I’m almost done with level 2!” Michael pleaded. “I can’t stop now. Five more minutes?”

“Why can’t video games be paused anymore?” his dad wondered. “I had no problem pausing when I was a kid.”

“Dad, if I stop now, I’ll lose my rank,” Michael explained.

“Well now, we wouldn’t want that, would we?” Dr. Gomez replied. “Okay, five more minutes.”

Video game time is a lot like football time and dog years—the 2-minute warning should really be the 20-minute warning, and a 10-year-old dog is 70. That’s why it was 9:15 before Dr. Gomez finally tucked Michael into bed. Michael and the squirrels prayed

and thanked God for a great day. Michael, of course, was thankful for his new video game, and Merle was thankful for getting to fly the drone. Pearl was thankful that Merle hadn't broken the drone.

"Oh," Dr. Gomez added after they had finished their prayers. "You'll be happy to know that Dr. Howard isn't interested in hearing anything else about Merle and Pearl. I brought them up again today at work, and he's convinced that I got too much sun and that 2,000-year-old talking squirrels are a figment of my imagination."

"I don't know why it's so hard to believe," Merle laughed.

"What it does mean, though, is that I'm off the hook for the time being, and you guys can stay," Dr. Gomez said.

"But we still need to be careful with the man in the suit and sunglasses. I don't think we've seen the last of him."

"We'll stay put and keep the alarm set," Pearl promised.

BLOOOING BLOOOING
PZHHHT!

CHAPTER 7

BLOOOING BLOOOING ZPHLTTT!

For the second night in a row, Pearl was awakened by a strange sound. She turned to Merle, who lay sleeping in the sawdust next to her, and gave him a gentle kick. "Merle!" she groaned. "That's disgusting."

"Not me," Merle replied groggily. He was telling the truth; he wasn't making the sounds. Pearl opened her eyes to see moonlight spilling into the room, giving away the facts that it was both very early in the morning and that Michael was not in his bed.

BLOOOING BLOOOING PZHHHT! BLOOOING BLOOOING ZPHLTTT!

The noises rang out again. "What is that?" Pearl wondered. She stepped out of her hamster mansion to investigate, creeping quietly through the bedroom door and into the hallway. The sounds grew louder as she approached the living room, her heart racing. Peeking slowly around the corner of the hallway, she discovered Michael, bathed in the flickering, cool light of his video game. "Michael?!" Pearl said.

"Huh?" Michael uttered, his drowsy eyes fixed on the television screen.

"The sun's not even up! What are you doing?"

"Getting through level 4," he mumbled.

"How long have you been awake?"

"I dunno. I got up early to play before school."

Merle, having missed out on the excitement the night before and not wanting to be left out this time, joined Michael and Pearl. "What'd I miss?" he wondered.

"Only a boy who should be sleeping." Pearl put her paws on her hips.

BLOP! BLING BLOOP BLOOM—SKAAAAAWISHHHHH!

"Yes!!!" Michael sat up straight. "I completed level 4!" He sank back into the sofa and closed his eyes. "I rule this game," he whispered.

"Hmm," Pearl pondered. "I was just wondering if this game was ruling *you*."

"What are you talking about?" Michael asked. "I just totally squished level 4."

"Yeah, what are you talking about?" Merle also wondered.

"You remember the Galatians, right, Merle?" Pearl asked.

"It's four in the morning." Merle yawned. "I can hardly remember my own name."

N
E
S
BLACK SE
GALATIA
AEGEAN SEA
MEDITERRANEAN SEA
ISRAE
TAP TAP

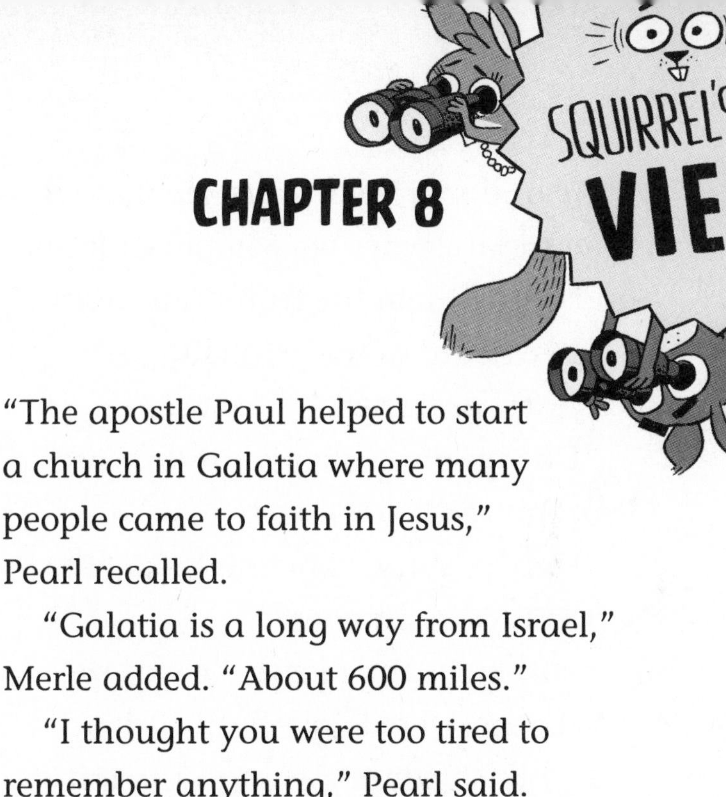

CHAPTER 8

"The apostle Paul helped to start a church in Galatia where many people came to faith in Jesus," Pearl recalled.

"Galatia is a long way from Israel," Merle added. "About 600 miles."

"I thought you were too tired to remember anything," Pearl said.

"It just came to me. I've got a memory for geography."

Pearl smiled and continued, "Paul sent a letter to the Galatian church to remind them that faith in Jesus is what saves them, not following rules. Paul also told the people that when God's Spirit lives in you, you will start to be more and more like Jesus. He named nine specific ways we will reflect Jesus and called them the fruit of the Spirit."

"I've heard of those in church," Michael confirmed.

"Do you remember what they are?" Pearl quizzed.

"Um . . . sorry," Michael said. "I'm kinda tired right now."

Pearl knew the reason he was tired was because he'd gotten up early to play, but she didn't want to rub it in.

"The first eight are love, joy, peace, patience, kindness, goodness, faithfulness, and gentleness. But the ninth one was the one *Super Squish Squids* made me think of."

"What's that one?" Michael wondered.

Pearl responded. "Sometimes the things we really want to do may not be the best things for us."

Michael frowned. "What's so bad

about wanting to do your best and win?"

"That's not bad on its own, but when it starts to get in the way of more important things, like sleep and school, it can be a problem. Over 1,000 years before Paul, King Solomon said, 'Better to be patient than powerful; better to have self-control than to conquer a city.'" Pearl paused a moment to let her words sink in. "Or conquer a video game."

Michael nodded his head groggily, then drifted off to sleep.

"Do you think he got that, Merle?" Pearl whispered. "Merle?"

"Zzzzz . . . ," Merle replied.

CHAPTER 9

"Getting up early to play video games is pretty much the same thing as staying up late to play them," Mrs. Gomez said as Michael sat down for breakfast. "Either way, you're not getting enough sleep."

"I feel fine," Michael insisted, rubbing at the bags under his eyes.

"Well, you look very tired. And you're not gonna do that again, understand?"

Michael sighed. "Yes, ma'am."

"Special delivery!" Justin announced, entering the kitchen carrying a large box.

"Good morning, Justin," Mrs. Gomez said.

"Whatcha got in the box?" Michael asked.

"I dunno," Justin replied. "It was on your doorstep. It's addressed to you."

Mrs. Gomez raised an eyebrow. "Odd for mail to arrive so early in the day."

But Michael was more than happy to receive an unexpected package. He wasted no time tearing open the box . . . to reveal a drone exactly like Edgar's.

"What?!" Michael wondered as Merle and Pearl entered the kitchen, munching on walnuts. "Suddenly my life is filled with drones?! This is so weird."

"Weird but awesome!" Merle said. "I suddenly have something fun to do today!" The squirrels would need to stay put in Michael's room since Mr. Nemesis, having been shut up in Jane's room the last two days, would have run of the house today. Staying locked in a room wasn't quite as bad as being stuck in a backpack all day, but it still made Merle feel very confined. "You take Edgar his drone back, and I'll make sure yours works!"

CHAPTER 10

DRONE!

Edgar demanded as he exited the bus, followed by his two lackeys, Pete and Bruce.

Michael handed over Edgar's drone and remote. Since Michael kept his end of the deal by bringing Edgar's drone back, Edgar kept up his end by not pounding Michael.

"Hey! It's broken!" Edgar complained, attempting to switch it on.

"It just needs to be recharged," Michael said quickly before Edgar could reconsider his end of the deal.

"By the way," Justin asked, "where did you get it?"

"I dunno." Edgar shrugged. "It just showed up. I must have a secret admirer."

Pete thought that was hilarious, which earned him a smack to the back of the head.

"Hmm. Okay," Michael replied. He decided not to tell Edgar he also had an admirer.

And Edgar decided not to tell Michael that his drone had come with a note that read "Use me to TP Michael Gomez's house!"

"Something fishy is going on with all these drones," Justin whispered to Michael as the boys headed down the hallway to class. Michael was about to agree when his attention suddenly turned to a more important topic.

"Level 5!" Sadie chirped as she walked past Michael and Justin.

"WHAT?!" Michael exclaimed, stopping cold in his tracks. "You got past level 5? No way!"

"Way!" Sadie countered, raising her arms in a touchdown signal.

Most kids, especially sleep-deprived ones, would have conceded defeat at this point, but not Michael. "She beat me in *Squish Squids 1* and *2*. I gotta win *3*, Justin!" Michael proclaimed, then yawned.

It didn't take long for Ms. McKay to throw a wrench in Michael's resolution. After reading the first chapter of *Treasure Island* in class, she assigned chapters 2 and 3 for homework. If you've ever read *Treasure Island*, you'll remember two things: one is that it's a great book about pirates (which Justin especially loved), and the other is that two chapters can take a serious bite out of video game playing time (which Michael especially *didn't* love).

CHAPTER 11

Speaking of great books, back at the Gomezes' house, Pearl was curled up reading a book she'd found on Michael's bookshelf, crying softly.

"Everything okay?" Merle asked, hearing her quiet sobs as he unplugged the drone from its charger.

"It's so beautiful." Pearl sniffed. "The spider is helping the pig."

"Really?" Merle wondered. "That's something I can't see myself getting emotional about."

"If you read it, you would understand," Pearl whimpered as she turned the page.

"All the lights are green, and I am

ready to go!" Merle proclaimed, rubbing his paws together. Having spent the whole morning watching the drone charge, he was bored out of his mind (unlike Pearl, who'd been keeping herself occupied with *Charlotte's Web*). Merle flipped a few switches, and building on what he'd learned the day before about drone piloting, was soon skillfully zipping the drone around the room.

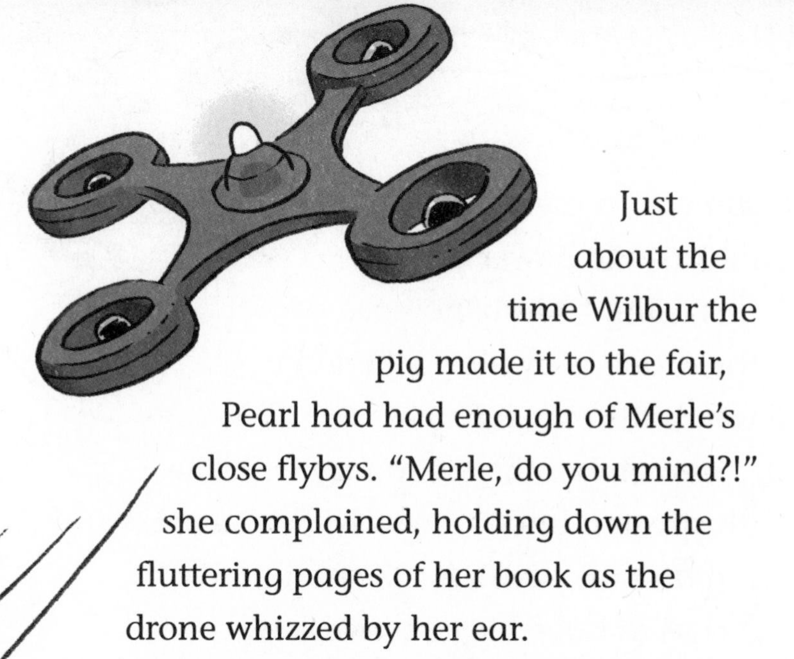

Just about the time Wilbur the pig made it to the fair, Pearl had had enough of Merle's close flybys. "Merle, do you mind?!" she complained, holding down the fluttering pages of her book as the drone whizzed by her ear.

"Do you suppose this thing could carry my weight?" Merle asked.

Pearl, sensing trouble, looked up from her book.

Merle knew that look. "I feel like I was born to fly, Pearl!" he explained.

"In real life, barn spiders don't spell. And tree squirrels don't fly."

"Why couldn't I?" Merle countered. "I'm telling you, Pearl, I'm sure I must have some flying squirrel in me. Plus, look at the power of this thing!" Merle hovered the drone at eye level. "I don't weigh that much!"

Remember the dictionary with the illustration under the word *persistence*? It didn't take long for Merle to make a case to have his picture added next to the 10-year-old who wants a video game. Pearl finally gave in and agreed to operate the remote.

"If you hurt yourself, it's not my fault," she warned.

"I'll be fine!" Merle assured her. "I can't fall very far in here."

Pearl looked up at the nine-foot ceilings. "I guess that's true."

Merle found a bandanna in Michael's dresser and attached it to the bottom of the drone, creating a seat for himself. He gave Pearl a quick lesson in operating the remote, and in no time, Merle was up and flying!

"Oops! Sorry! Sorry!" Pearl apologized as Merle bumped off furniture and walls while she tried to get the hang of the remote.

"HA HA HA HA! No problem—I'm great! I can't remember the last time I had so much fun!" Merle laughed as Pearl hovered the drone in front of the bedroom door.

At that very moment, however, Michael, returning home from school, opened the door with a jolt, sending Merle and the drone flying across the room. They banged into a wall and landed with a thud on Michael's bed.

"Woo-hoo! Still okay!" Merle squealed.

CHAPTER 12

Michael tossed his backpack on his desk and immediately headed back out the door.

"Where are you going?" Pearl wondered. "Don't you have homework?"

"Just a little reading," Michael answered over his shoulder. "I've got a plan. I'm going to play *Super Squish Squids* first and then read before bed!" Mysteriously, somewhere on his walk between school and home, two chapters of *Treasure Island* had turned into *just a little reading*. Some of the best-laid plans of 10-year-old boys can succeed only at the expense of reality. Michael took off toward the living room, forgetting to close his bedroom door behind him.

"Merle, we need to close the door before the cat comes in," Pearl cautioned as Merle took the drone remote from her paws.

"Hold on," Merle said. He scurried back to the bed, where the drone sat. "I have another idea." Merle climbed back into his bandanna seat and powered up the craft. "I wonder if the drone can handle my weight plus the weight of the remote?" Merle rose off the bed with ease and sailed out the door. "And the answer is yes!"

"Merle!" Pearl hollered, running after him.

The buzzing of the drone in the hallway caught Mr. Nemesis's attention right away, and the chase was on! As Michael systematically squished squids, Merle had a ball tormenting the cat. Like a kitten trying to catch the light of a laser pointer, Mr. Nemesis was no match for Merle's fast-improving piloting skills.

"Here kitty, kitty, kitty!" Merle taunted, hovering just above Mr. Nemesis's head. By the time the

poor cat was able to react, Merle had zipped up into the corner of the living room, safely out of reach. "Haha!" Merle giggled with glee.

"You'll be sorry if he catches you!" Pearl warned.

"Maybe!" Merle said, doing a loop the loop. "But this is so much fun, I just can't help myself!"

"Yes! Level 5!" Michael exclaimed as he jumped up from the sofa to do a victory dance.

Pearl shook her head at the chaotic scene. "Not being able to help yourself seems to be a common theme at the moment."

CHAPTER 13

Three things won't surprise you. The first is that Michael didn't leave himself enough time to read before bed. That, combined with the fact that he'd been sleepy all day to begin with, meant that what he *did* read didn't sink in. By the time he drifted off, he couldn't have told you the difference between Black Dog and Billy Bones.

"How'd your reading go?" Justin asked cheerfully as he entered the Gomezes' kitchen the next day, carrying another package.

"Okay, I guess," Michael fibbed between bites of Cocoa Fluffies. "What's in the box?"

"Another package at your door." Justin shook the box. "I bet it's a drone!"

Because the package was the exact same size and weight as the first one, Justin's guess wasn't much of a stretch. Sure enough, it was another drone.

"This is nuts! Who is sending all these drones? Have you gotten any?" Michael asked.

"I wish," Justin replied.

"Well, you can borrow one from me sometime if you want," Michael offered as the boys headed out for school.

The second thing that won't surprise you is that Michael had a terrible day at school. Not only did he learn that Sadie was now *two* levels ahead of him in *Super Squish Squids,* but the class discussion of *Treasure Island* was a disaster.

"One of the main themes in the book is introduced early on," Ms. McKay said to the class. "Who can tell me what it might be?"

I don't know how they do it, but teachers always seem to know who did and didn't do the homework just by looking. Maybe it's the kids avoiding eye contact who give themselves away.

"Michael!" Ms. McKay called out. "What do you think?"

Michael's memory was a confused jumble of squids, drones, and pirates.

After trying his best to remember anything at all about what he'd read, all he could come up with was, "Um . . . treasure?"

The third thing that won't surprise you is that *treasure* was not the correct answer.

"Self-control?" Justin answered correctly.

"Or, the lack thereof. Good job, Justin!" Ms. McKay beamed at Justin as Michael sank down in his chair.

CHAPTER 14

Merle discovered the second drone on the kitchen table shortly after Michael and Justin left for school. He had yet to experience Christmas, since it was currently September, and he had been frozen in a cave for 300 years before the holiday's first official celebration. But finding a second drone in as many days felt a lot like Christmas to Merle.

"Would you look at this?!" he marveled to Pearl. "A matching set!"

"What are you going to do with two drones?" Pearl asked.

"One for me, and one for you!" Merle responded. Like cycling, it's

much more fun when you ride with friends.

"No way!" Pearl stated.

"C'mon!" he pleaded. "The cat's in Jane's room today. We can fly around the whole house. You'll love it!"

It took Merle a while to talk Pearl into being his flying partner (conveniently, about the same amount of time it took to charge the new drone). But by noon the two were zipping through the halls of the house, and Pearl was having the time of her life.

"Wheeeee!" Pearl giggled. "This is almost as much fun as roller-skating!"

Merle and Pearl played follow-the-leader through the hallway from the bedrooms, into the living room, and around the kitchen.

"What do you mean, 'almost'?" Merle shouted over the buzz of the drone propellers. "Flying beats skating by a mile!"

"But skating comes with music!" Pearl responded, which gave Merle an idea. He buzzed by the living room stereo and clicked it on, filling the house with classic hits from the '80s. "Okay, now it's better!" Pearl admitted with a huge grin.

With several loops around the house under his belt, Merle was up for more of a challenge. Both he and Pearl were quickly turning into top-notch pilots.

"What do you say we go for a spin outside?" Merle suggested.

Pearl slammed on the air brakes, shocked at the suggestion. "Merle, we can't go outside. You heard what Dr. Gomez said. It's too dangerous."

"Oh, come on, Pearl! If I can keep

away from a cat in a tight space, I can avoid any squirrelnappers in the great outdoors!"

"Merle . . . ," Pearl appealed, but it was too late. Her husband disarmed the alarm on a quick flyby and headed for Michael's bedroom window.

"I'm telling you, Pearl, I can't help myself—I was born to fly!!!"

CHAPTER 15

Michael's bedroom window slid open, and Merle sailed outside. He zipped high above the houses and treetops, looking down on the world below. He had never been this high up! "Whoa—this is amazing!" he shouted.

Bob, Mary, and Larry heard the buzz of the drone and Merle's shout and came out of their tree houses to investigate.

"I didn't know you were a flying squirrel, Merle!" Larry hollered. "My cousin can fly too!" Larry did, in fact, have a flying squirrel cousin in North Carolina.

"Technically, that's more of a glide! *This* is flying!" Merle boasted as he performed a giant loop the loop, followed by a climbing corkscrew and a two-point roll.

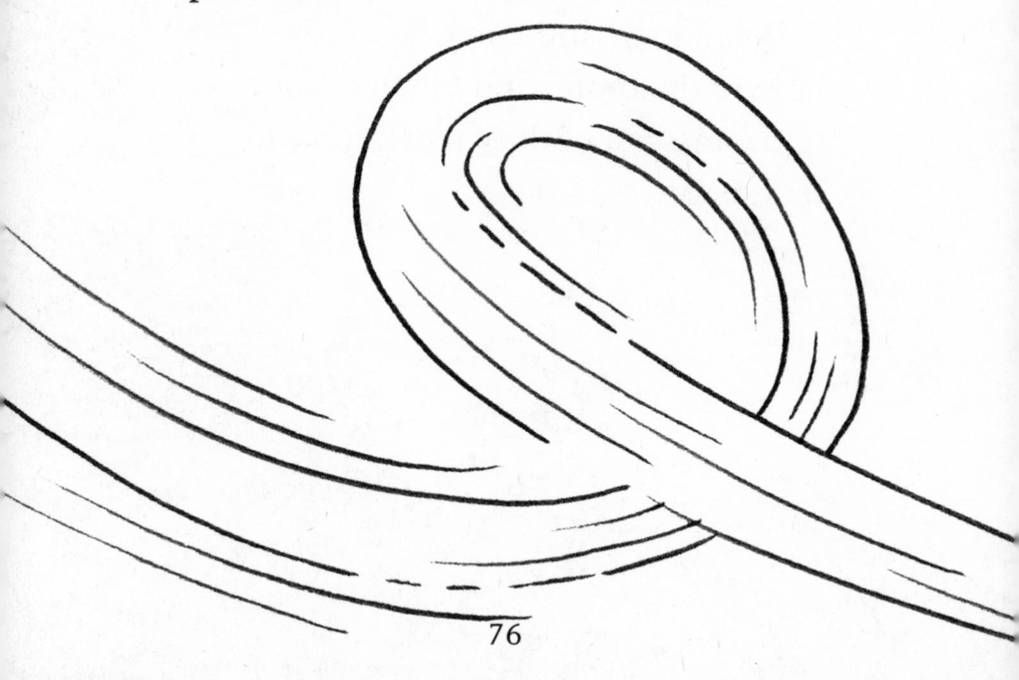

The three Tennessee squirrels cheered and applauded Merle's aerobatics.

Pearl popped her head out of the window. "Merle! Be careful!" she called out.

"Don't worry, Pearl!" Merle called back. "I'm fine! This couldn't get any better!"

It turns out that Merle was only partly correct. He was right that things couldn't get any better—because they got immediately worse! But he was very wrong about being fine! Merle suddenly lost control over the drone.

When he tried to zip left, he somehow moved right.

"Huh?" he uttered as he tried to move left *again* but kept going straight.

"Where you goin', Merle?!" Bob yelled.

"I'm trying to—" Merle paused in horror at the sight below him. About a half mile in the distance stood the man in the suit and sunglasses beside his white car. He was operating a remote that seemed to be overriding Merle's, controlling the drone! Merle was like a helpless fish being reeled in to shore after taking the bait!

Because she was close to the ground, Pearl couldn't see what Merle saw. "What's happening?!" she called up to Bob.

"HELP!!!" Merle cried.

CHAPTER 16

Bob ran up to the very top of his tree to get a better look. "Merle's flying toward a man in a suit!" he reported down to Pearl.

Pearl's heart sank. "Is he wearing sunglasses?" she shouted back up.

"Yes! How did you know?"

Pearl needed to think fast. Michael, Mrs. Gomez, and Jane were still at school. Dr. Gomez was still at work. "What do I do? What do I do?!" She looked back over her shoulder into Michael's bedroom and saw the drone she had been piloting. Taking a deep breath, she scurried from the windowsill back into the room.

"Where are you going?" Bob called out. "Merle's going the other way!"

Merle, in his drone prison, was getting closer and closer to the man in the suit and sunglasses. His remote was useless. Merle's only way to escape was to jump, but he was way too high.

"I wish I were *Glaucomys volans*!" Merle cried, recalling the scientific name for the Southern flying squirrel. "Gliding now would be just fine!!!"

WHRRRRR! Pearl, piloting her drone, zipped out of the window, racing toward Merle.

"Yeah!" cheered the Tennessee squirrels.

At that moment, Michael, returning home from school, turned the corner onto his street. Hearing drone engines, he looked up and saw Pearl.

"Pearl?!" he shouted. "What are you doing?!"

"I'm saving Merle!" she shouted back. Suddenly, Pearl's look of determination turned to terror as she realized she no longer had control over her craft. She, too, was being reeled in by the man in the suit and sunglasses!

she screamed.

“What’s happening?!” Michael called out, not able to see the man from his vantage point.

The Tennessee squirrels made a terrible racket shouting down at Michael, trying to tell him what was happening. Unfortunately, Michael did not speak squirrel and so made out only a cacophony of panicky squeaks.

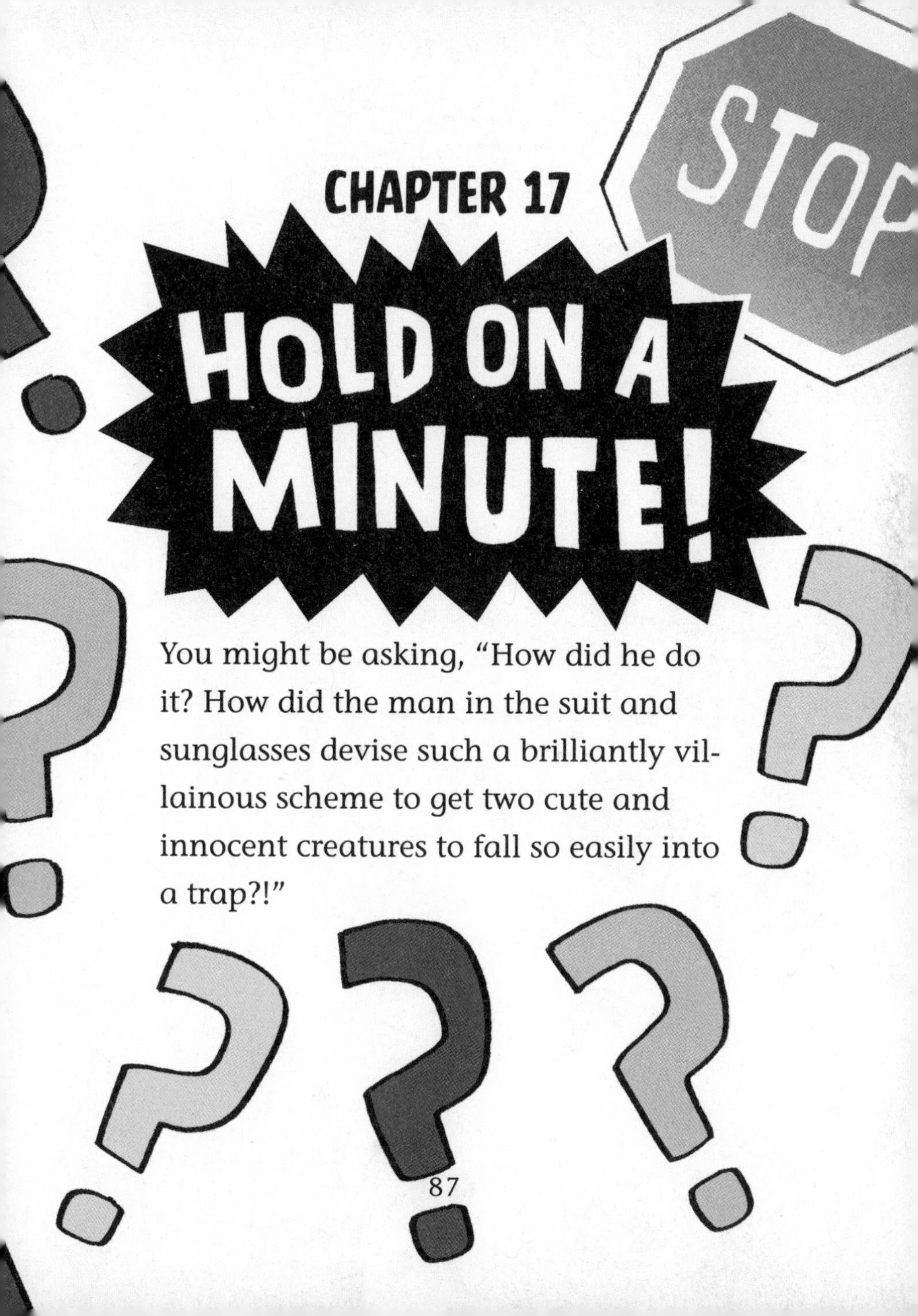

CHAPTER 17

HOLD ON A MINUTE!

You might be asking, "How did he do it? How did the man in the suit and sunglasses devise such a brilliantly villainous scheme to get two cute and innocent creatures to fall so easily into a trap?!"

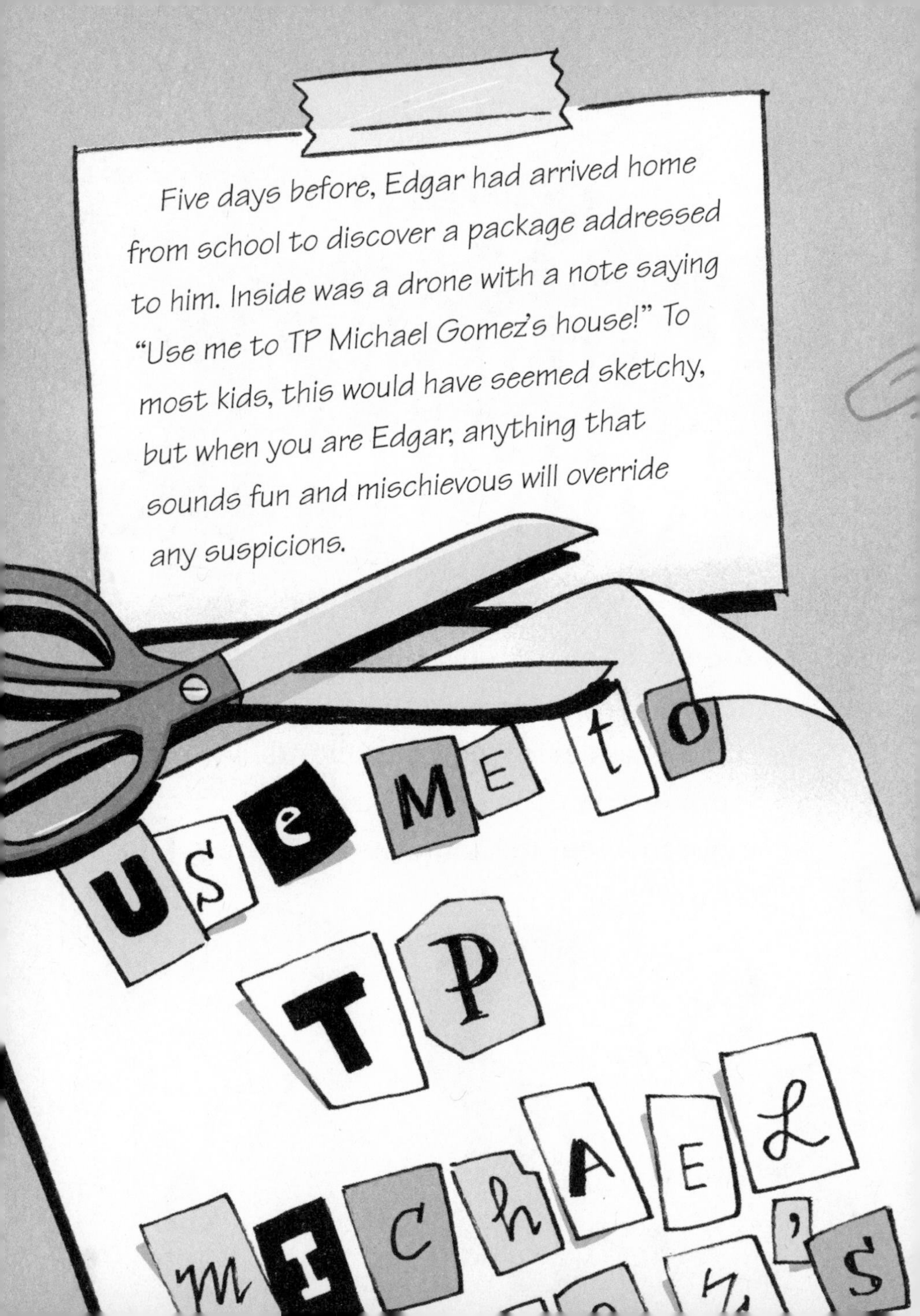
Five days before, Edgar had arrived home from school to discover a package addressed to him. Inside was a drone with a note saying "Use me to TP Michael Gomez's house!" To most kids, this would have seemed sketchy, but when you are Edgar, anything that sounds fun and mischievous will override any suspicions.
USeMEto
TP
mIChAEL'S

The man in the suit and sunglasses had gathered enough information about the squirrels by this point to know that Merle had a soft spot for gadgets. Any squirrel that would build his own raft to sail down the Jordan or take so quickly to roller-skating would surely love to operate a drone. And any squirrel adventurous enough to explore an uncharted cave would surely figure out a way to fly in a drone! And surely it wouldn't be long before flying indoors wasn't good enough, and the squirrel would venture outside! Simply put, the man in the suit and sunglasses was counting on Merle not being able to help himself!

The only question that remained was how to get Merle a drone. It would be too suspicious to just deliver one to Michael's house. But if the man in the suit and sun-glasses gave one to Edgar first, no one would deduce the drone was from him! And once Michael knew someone had given Edgar a drone, the man could pepper Merle with drones, and no one would be the wiser!
YOU GET A DRONE!
AND YOU!
AND YOU!
AND YOU!
OH! AND YOU!

CATCH 1
The man in the suit and sunglasses's plan had worked perfectly! Merle's lack of self-control had allowed the man to nab not only Merle but Pearl, too!
GET 1 FREE

CHAPTER 18

PEARL!

Michael yelled, sprinting down the street while attempting to follow her flight path.

"He's got Merle!" Pearl shouted. "And he's controlling my drone!"

Michael climbed over their neighbor, Mr. Phillips's, fence, running through his backyard to keep track of Pearl.

"Who's got Merle!?" he asked, though he feared he already knew the answer.

"The man in the suit and sunglasses!" Pearl screamed as she disappeared over the rooftops.

By the time Michael had hopped enough fences and run through enough yards to make it to where the white Toyota had been parked, the man in the suit and sunglasses, along with Merle and Pearl, was long gone.

"I told you to not go outside!" Pearl complained in the darkness.

"Hey, you know what's funny? The last time we were trapped in the pitch-black was after you warned me to not go *inside*!" Merle joked, referring to the time nearly 2,000 years before when Pearl had warned him to not venture into the cave by the Dead Sea.

"I actually don't think that's funny at all," Pearl replied sternly.

"I know, I know." Merle patted around in the dark until he found Pearl's paw. "I'm so sorry, Pearl. I couldn't control myself."

Pearl sniffed. "You mean you *didn't* control yourself."

"I was *remote*-controlling myself," Merle quipped sheepishly.

"Also not funny."

The white Toyota, driven by the man in the suit and sunglasses, with two 2,000-year-old talking squirrels in the trunk, made its way down the interstate toward the airport.

CHAPTER 19

"What are we going to do, Dad?!" Michael asked Dr. Gomez as the family gathered in Michael's room for bedtime prayers. Next to Michael's bed sat Merle and Pearl's empty hamster mansion. The family sat solemnly, waiting for Dr. Gomez's response.

"I don't know, buddy," he finally admitted. "There's no telling where they are now." Of course, they had checked the hotel where they had last seen the man in the suit and sunglasses, as well as with the rental car company where he'd rented his car, but had come up empty.

"I hope they don't go back to the

Dead Sea," Jane said sadly. Mr. Nemesis purred happily in her lap. In contrast with the rest of the family, the cat seemed quite content with the current state of affairs. Without Merle and Pearl, he had the house and the family all to himself again.

"Why did the squirrels leave the house if they knew that man was after them?" Mrs. Gomez asked.

"Merle loved that drone," Michael answered. "He was having so much fun he said he just couldn't help himself." No sooner had the words left his mouth than Michael realized Merle's flying fascination wasn't too different from his obsession with *Super Squish Squids*. "I get it," he admitted. "I've been so focused on beating Sadie at *Super Squids 3* that I've also been having trouble controlling myself."

"All of us have weaknesses," his mom said, ruffling his hair. "God can use the things we struggle with to remind us of our need for his help."

Michael prayed and asked God for his fruit of the Spirit of self-control. "Thank you for your love for me when I need it the most, and please help me to trust you for everything in my life," he said. The family then prayed for Merle and Pearl and for their safe return.

As Mrs. Gomez, Jane, and Mr. Nemesis exited Michael's room, Dr. Gomez picked up the backpack Michael had used to bring Merle and Pearl home to Tennessee and set it next to Michael's bed.

"Get some sleep, buddy," Dr. Gomez said. "We need to find Merle and Pearl. Their knowledge is too valuable, and they can't end up in the wrong hands. We'll pack in the morning."

MICHAEL GOMEZ is an adventurous and active 10-year-old boy. He is kindhearted but often acts before he thinks. He's friendly and talkative and blissfully unaware that most of his classmates think he's a bit geeky. Michael is super excited to be in fifth grade, which, in his mind, makes him "grade school royalty!"

MERLE SQUIRREL may be thousands of years old, but he never really grew up. He has endless enthusiasm for anything new and interesting—especially this strange modern world he finds himself in. He marvels at the self-refilling bowl of fresh drinking water (otherwise known as a toilet) and supplements his regular diet of tree nuts with what he believes might be the world's most perfect food: chicken nuggets. He's old enough to know better, but he often finds it hard to do better. Good thing he's got his wife, Pearl, to help him make wise choices.

PEARL SQUIRREL is wise beyond her many, many, many years, with enough common sense for both her and Merle. When Michael's in a bind, she loves to share a lesson or bit of wisdom from Bible events she witnessed in her youth. Pearl's biggest quirk is that she is a nut hoarder. Having come from a world where food is scarce, her instinct is to grab whatever she can. The abundance and variety of nuts in present-day Tennessee can lead to distraction and storage issues.

CHARACTER PROFILE

JUSTIN KESSLER is Michael's best friend. Justin is quieter and has better judgment than Michael, and he is super smart. He's a rule follower and is obsessed with being on time. He'll usually give in to what Michael wants to do after warning him of the likely consequences.

CHARACTER PROFILE

SADIE HENDERSON is Michael and Justin's other best friend. She enjoys video games and bowling just as much as cheerleading and pajama parties. She gets mad respect from her classmates as the only kid at Walnut Creek Elementary who's not afraid of school bully Edgar. Though Sadie's in a different homeroom than her two best friends, the three always sit together at lunch and hang out after class.

CHARACTER PROFILE

DR. GOMEZ, a professor of anthropology, is not thrilled when he finds out that his son, Michael, smuggled two ancient squirrels home from their summer trip to the Dead Sea, but he ends up seeing great value in having them around as original sources for his research. Dad loves his son's adventurous spirit but wishes Michael would look (or at least peek) before he leaps.

CHARACTER PROFILE

MRS. GOMEZ teaches part-time at her daughter's preschool and is a full-time mom to Michael and Jane. She feels sorry for the fish-out-of-water squirrels and looks for ways to help them feel at home, including constructing and decorating an over-the-top hamster mansion for Merle and Pearl in Michael's room. She also can't help but call Michael by her favorite (and his least favorite) nickname, Cookies.

MR. NEMESIS is the Gomez family cat who becomes Merle and Pearl's true nemesis. Jealous of the time and attention given to the squirrels by his family, Mr. Nemesis is continuously coming up with brilliant and creative ways to get rid of them. He hides his ability to talk from the family, but not the squirrels.

JANE GOMEZ is Michael's little sister. She's super adorable but delights in getting her brother busted so she can be known as the "good child." She thinks Merle and Pearl are the cutest things she has ever seen in her whole life (next to Mr. Nemesis) and is fond of dressing them up in her doll clothes.

DR. GOMEZ'S
Historical Handbook

So now you've heard of the Dead Sea Squirrels, but what about the

DEAD SEA *SCROLLS*?

Way back in 1946, just after the end of World War II, in a cave along the banks of the Dead Sea, a 15-year-old boy came across some jars containing ancient scrolls while looking after his goats. When scholars and archaeologists found out about his discovery, the hunt for more scrolls was on! Over the next 10 years, many more scrolls and pieces of scrolls were found in 11 different caves.

There are different theories about exactly who wrote on the scrolls and hid them in the caves. One of the most popular ideas is that they belonged to a group of Jewish priests called Essenes, who lived in the desert because they had been thrown out of Jerusalem. One thing is for sure—the scrolls are very, very old! They were placed in the caves between the years 300 BC and AD 100!

Forty percent of the words on the scrolls come from the Bible. Parts of every Old Testament book except for the book of Esther have been discovered.

Of the remaining 60 percent, half are religious texts not found in the Bible, and half are historical records about the way people lived 2,000 years ago.

The discovery of the Dead Sea Scrolls is one of the most important archaeological finds in history!

About the Author

As co-creator of VeggieTales, co-founder of Big Idea Entertainment, and the voice of the beloved Larry the Cucumber, **MIKE NAWROCKI** has been dedicated to helping parents pass on biblical values to their kids through storytelling for over two decades. Mike currently serves as assistant professor of film and animation at Lipscomb University in Nashville, Tennessee, and makes his home in nearby Franklin with his wife, Lisa, and their two children. The Dead Sea Squirrels is Mike's first children's book series.

Don't go nuts waiting to find out what happens to

Get the next book today!

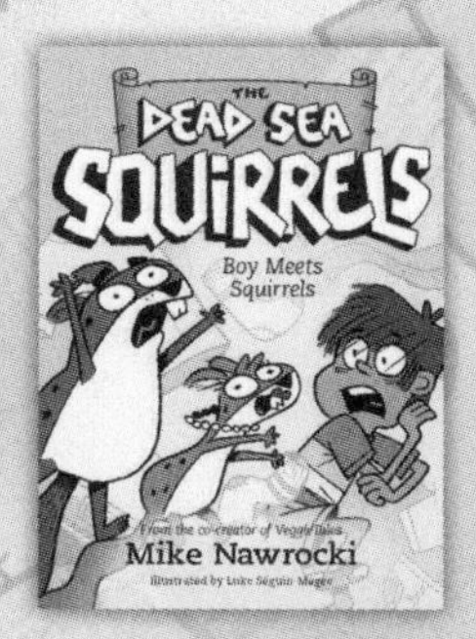

Watch out for more adventures with Merle, Pearl, and all their friends!

CP1478